mini saga
competition 2007

for Primary Schools from Young Writers in association with

tiny tales

South East England

First published in Great Britain in 2007 by
Young Writers, Remus House, Coltsfoot Drive,
Peterborough, PE2 9JX
Tel (01733) 890066 Fax (01733) 313524
All Rights Reserved

© Copyright Contributors 2007
SB ISBN 978-1-84431-301-3

Foreword

Young Writers was established in 1991, with the aim of encouraging the children and young adults of today to think and write creatively. Our latest primary school competition, *Tiny Tales*, posed an exciting challenge for these young authors: to write, in no more than fifty words, a story encompassing a beginning, a middle and an end. We call this the mini saga.

Tiny Tales South East England is our latest offering from the wealth of young talent that has mastered this incredibly challenging form. With such an abundance of imagination, humour and ability evident in such a wide variety of stories, these young writers cannot fail to enthral and excite with every tale.

Contents

Carlton Hill Primary School,
Brighton

Copthorne Preparatory School,
Copthorne

Great Rollright Primary School,
Chipping Norton

Haslemere Preparatory School,
Haslemere

Whiteley Primary School, Fareham

The Mini Sagas

Roller Coasters

My hands trembled as I climbed into a loop the loop roller coaster. Mum said it would be fun, but I didn't believe her. I was dreading it. It started; first it went slow, then it went fast and then it suddenly came to an end. It had finally finished!

Hannah French (9)
Babington House School, Chislehurst

13

The Spell Book

A prince returned home. A ball was held in his honour. As the servants cleaned, they discovered a spell book. Suddenly, there was a loud roar from a dragon. The servants opened the spell book, recited a spell and the dragon disappeared. Everyone in the kingdom lived happily ever after.

Alex Green (8)
Babington House School, Chislehurst

The Angry Robbers

There were angry robbers around the town and they wanted money. They got in and robbed the castle. They found a locked room and started looking for the key; they found it and went in. When they were in there, they found a book. It said *danger* on the front.

Isabelle French (9)
Babington House School, Chislehurst

15

The Sweetie Shop

One day a little girl called Emma went down the road to buy some sweets. When she got there, there was a queue, so she waited in the queue for some candy, but when it was her turn, she realised she did not have enough money. Emma walked home upset.

Bibiana Brown (9)
Babington House School, Chislehurst

It's Gone!

It was gone! The golden watch my grandmother gave me was gone! I searched through my drawers, old homework papers and banana skins came flying out behind me. I was about to give up, when I heard footsteps. I turned round. There it was, it wasn't there before, was it?

Georgia Pactat (10)
Barrow Hills School, Godalming

17

The Solar System

I've always wanted to fly up to space and I woke up one morning and thought this would be the day. I asked Mum and knowing mums, she said, 'No! Who do you think you are?' I ignored her and got out my astronaut suit and rocket. Up I went.

Chloë Fitzsimons (10)
Barrow Hills School, Godalming

What's That?

The silence was deafening. The rain battered
on the window. The light flickered and
eventually went out with a hiss. Suddenly, I
got scared. I heard a creak. The creaking got
nearer, my heart was racing.
'The power's off, here's a candle.'
I jumped. I muttered, 'Oh, it's you Mum!'

Alana Hopkins (10)
Barrow Hills School, Godalming

Fight

Angry bullets whizzed past. The Orcs were attacking from the rear. The Space Marines opened fire. Arnias Calgar was shouting orders. Orcs were being massacred. A Dreadnought came lumbering out of the smoke and fired a hailstorm of burning rockets. The tide was turning. The Space Marines had won!

Harry Clough (10)
Barrow Hills School, Godalming

Oops!

Alien Zog was on a voyage to Planet Zing. Suddenly, there was an explosion. He crashed into a shed on Planet Earth. His ship damaged, he sees lots of strange objects. Zog stepped on something sharp. He jumped back surprised, knocking over his ship. Lights flashed and Zog was away.

Ben Hanlan (9)
Barrow Hills School, Godalming

Rough Sleeper

The evil aliens were approaching. They had slime guns and seven eyes. Why did they want my diamond ring?
'Die boy, die!'
Oh no, I am James Bond, the only person who can save us!
'Help me!' I shout.
'Dave, Dave, wake up, time for school!' said Mum hastily.

India Phillips (10)
Barrow Hills School, Godalming

The Hat

When Tom woke up one morning, he went downstairs and saw that the closet door was open. So he went to close it, but something caught his eye and it was a really weird hat. So he picked it up and put it on his head. Something weird happened.

Corry De Candole (10)
Barrow Hills School, Godalming

True Love

Her beauty was off the scale; her eyes pinned me down; I knew it was love at first sight. Her skin glowed from within; her face was more beautiful than the Cistine Chapel. Then my wife gently said, 'George darling, what are we going to call our new daughter?'

Justin Gonsalves (10)
Barrow Hills School, Godalming

The Haunted House

I was on a walk in the dark, scary woods, when I came across an unusual house. It reminded me of the haunted house I'd seen on TV. I decided to go inside. I turned the handle. As I stepped inside, the huge door slammed behind me. I felt terrified!

Lucy Pierce (10)
Barrow Hills School, Godalming

The Gruesome Dentist

Betty Buckworth went to get her braces done. She walked into the revolting room, sat down and opened her mouth. The dentist said, 'Betty, shut your eyes and don't open them until I say!' However, guess what happened? She opened them and nobody knows what happened to Betty Buckworth!

Georgia Bousfield (10)
Barrow Hills School, Godalming

The Fantastic Wizard

There was a wizard called Hackeldodle. He didn't know how to do magic, so he went to a magic university. He learned a lot at the university, like cooking, gardening and of course, magic. After a couple of years, he became a mage and made himself disappear into space.

Alexander J Coates (10)
Barrow Hills School, Godalming

The Chase

'Stop right there, boy! We saw you steal from
the corner shop. You will go back and pay for
the things you stole, or you will be charged!'
I went back to the shop and paid for the things I
stole. I went home and told my mum and dad.

David Ellis (10)
Barrow Hills School, Godalming

Lost In The Mountains

Louise and I were skiing alone that day. Being up the mountain was like being on top of the world. Suddenly, we realised we were alone. Where was everyone? We were lost, alone and now very frightened. We searched, but couldn't find our way home. Would we find it?

Francesca Vallini (10)
Barrow Hills School, Godalming

The Chest

Once I went shopping with my friends in Godalming, when we saw a pathway. We walked down it and all the walls went cold. India got scared and ran off, but I stayed. At the end was a chest. It was open. We looked inside and there was real gold!

Ruby Woods (10)
Barrow Hills School, Godalming

The Ground Doomer

The ground shook violently. I was scared.
'It's the Ground Doomer causing an
earthquake,' said an old man. 'There is a myth,
thousands of years before our race, far away
galaxies were destroyed by fire. He's here to
scorch us!'
Suddenly, there was a crack in the ground
under me.

Guy Andrews (10)
Barrow Hills School, Godalming

The Dark Cave

The cave looked dark and gloomy. Sarah
began to panic. She said quietly, 'Are we ever
going to get out of here?'
Her best friend answered, 'Of course we are.'
They heard footsteps behind them. They
quickly hid, but they weren't quick enough.
'Found you! everyone's looking for you!'

Ruth Rigby (11)
Barrow Hills School, Godalming

Doughnut

Bald and dumb, Homer Simpson has eaten half a doughnut. It crashes to the floor. His skinny, fast dog grabs it so fast, Homer could not get it again. Bart zooms down the stairs on his skateboard and crashes into the dog, who drops the doughnut!

Joshua Pratt (10)
Bishop Loveday CE Primary School, Banbury

Gobbolino, The Witch's Cat

Gobbolino the witch's cat finds he has one white paw and gets kicked out of the dark, gloomy cavern. He ventures into a town and gets battered, so he jumps on the roofs and goes down a chimney and lands in a palace and stays there forever and ever.

Max Parkhouse (10)
Bishop Loveday CE Primary School, Banbury

Dr Who And The Monster

'Mather, don't look!'
But Mather looked at the dreaded monster and fainted.
'Mather!' shouted the Doctor, trying to wake her. He heard noises.
'It's you,' said a voice. It was the Daleks.
'I never did any harm to your Dalek empire, you did!'
'Argh!' Mather yelled in fright when awoken.

Abbie Harris (10)
Bishop Loveday CE Primary School, Banbury

The Death of Obi Wan

Annakin Skywalker had turned to the dark side and he is fighting Obi Wan, who is a Jedi. Obi Wan jumped high and was just about to land, when he was stabbed by Annakin.
Obi Wan had been killed by his evil apprentice.

Jack Marsh (10)
Bishop Loveday CE Primary School, Banbury

Fairy Dust

Rosie loses her tartan sock and checks everywhere. One night a little fairy borrows it. Her room is very tidy, but a particular fairy is hiding in her sock. At last, the tiny fairy casts a spell to make the sock come back into her room.

Katy Baker (10)
Bishop Loveday CE Primary School, Banbury

Dinosaur Dream

He lay still, he didn't want to move, he might get stood on by a T-rex. Tom stared at a baby T-rex wondering if he could ride on it. He started to ride but he got attacked by the mum T-rex. 'Get out of bed right this moment Tom!'

Aaron Baker (10)
Bishop Loveday CE Primary School, Banbury

Lady And The Tramp 2

'No!' shouted Tramp's parents. Tramp got fed
up with sticking to rules and getting punished.
He had to stay out in the garden for the night.
Then Tramp jumped over the crooked fence
and ran away.
It was morning and Tramp was beginning to get
worried. Suddenly, he spotted Dad.

Indya Clayton (10)
Bishop Loveday CE Primary School, Banbury

Big Experiment

One lovely summer's day, Alice and her mum were having a picnic. Alice then decided to go for a walk. She fell through a sinking trap and found herself in a lab. The professor was making an experiment and threw it in the air. Alice then turned a pale pink.

Darcy Hawtin (10)
Bishop Loveday CE Primary School, Banbury

The Spooky Old Ghost

One spooky night in an old haunted house, lived Jae and a spooky old ghost. The ghost put spiders in Jae's bed and scared him to death.

Mum shouted, 'Get out of bed, it 's time for school!'

Jack Fisher (10)
Bishop Loveday CE Primary School, Banbury

Home Alone

Bye Mum and bye Dad … *yes* they have gone.
Good! Home alone. Right, checklist. TV remote,
popcorn, scary movies and sofa den. Right,
'Dead Man's Back' that sounds scary enough
for me! Lights out! *Argh!* What's that noise? Oh,
it's Mum and Dad opening the door.
'Hello! Night, night!'

Jessica Holder (10)
Bishop Loveday CE Primary School, Banbury

The Monster Story In 50 Words

He lay on the stone-cold floor with a monster somewhere around him. The monster grew close. He could feel it. He heard it stomping around the corner. The monster leant over him to kill him. Then Max woke up and realised it was just a dream.

Katrina Edmunds (10)
Bishop Loveday CE Primary School, Banbury

Stuck

There I was, stuck in slime, from head to toe, waiting silently, but then a very weird thing happened. Growing out from the slime was a monster!
Suddenly, I found myself sinking. I took a deep breath and went down into a very dark dungeon and starved to death.

Megan Woodruff (10)
Bishop Loveday CE Primary School, Banbury

Alice In Wonderland

Following the white rabbit down a hole, Alice finds herself lost in a beautiful garden. Meeting the Queen of Hearts, Alice has to play croquet with the Queen or she'll be beheaded.
She woke up on the riverbank, holding a pack of cards. *What a curious dream,* she thought.

Lucy Harper (10)
Bishop Loveday CE Primary School, Banbury

The Scary Monster!

Creep, creep, creep, sweat was dripping down my back. The door started creaking. The monster pounced on me and started doing something to me. I screamed. I looked down at the monster and I saw it was just my dog.

Jessica Reynolds (10)
Bishop Loveday CE Primary School, Banbury

The Journey

Suddenly, my heart started pounding and then I felt the wind get faster and faster. I didn't know what to do, but it started to slow down and the tight, silver bar came up and someone put their hand out to get me from the roller coaster.

Troy Dixon (10)
Bishop Loveday CE Primary School, Banbury

The Early Bird

Last week, I woke up at my normal time and slowly got out of bed. I looked at the clock. It was later than I thought. I ran about, getting ready.
As I legged it into school, no one was there. I realised my clock was an hour too fast.

Hannah Macey (10)
Bishop Loveday CE Primary School, Banbury

The Scary Monster

Creep, creep, creep, the sweat was dripping down my back. The door started creeping open. The monster slid in.
Suddenly, it pounced on me and started licking me. Then I screamed. I reached for my light. Then I looked down. The monster was my dog.

Rosalind McDermid-Perring (9)
Bishop Loveday CE Primary School, Banbury

End Of The World

Beads of sweat were dripping from his face, his shirt was clinging onto his back, his hands were trembling, the last sound he would ever hear, would be the world blowing up! *Ding!* Phew! He was still alive! David always dreaded warming up his soup!

Diba Farahmand-Razavi (10)
Bishop Loveday CE Primary School, Banbury

Dog Shock

I was in bed, the quilt tucked tightly over my head. The door was making a scratching noise, so I got up and sped to the door and opened the door. Suddenly, a dog burst through the door, barking its head off.

Christopher Lewis (9)
Bishop Loveday CE Primary School, Banbury

Shock!

My knees were shaking. My head was throbbing. Then suddenly my stomach lurched. My body was pushed back, we were off! The rally car was amazing. Why should I have been so scared?

Thomas Dence (9)
Bishop Loveday CE Primary School, Banbury

The Deadly Fall

I was cold and wet, I tripped, I fell, the whole world was spinning right in front of me. It felt as if I was going to die.

Then suddenly, someone came up behind me and shouted, 'Stuck.'

All that had happened was that someone had stuck me in a game.

Georgia England (10)
Bishop Loveday CE Primary School, Banbury

The Adventures Of Apple Man And Bicycle Boy

In the apple lair, Bicycle Boy and Apple Man were playing snooker. Just then, the police gave them a ring.
The Robohobo Monkey shrank Apple Man and Bicycle Boy. Apple Man held onto the Robohobo Monkey and turned him off.

Rory Heaverman (10)
Bishop Loveday CE Primary School, Banbury

The Graveyard At Night

I stood alone in the dark graveyard. I shivered, terrified. An owl watched me, its eyes glowing bright. It began to rain. I heard a rustle in the bushes. What was it, a bear? I turned around, scared, but it was a tiny little grey cat!

Ellie Macey (10)
Bishop Loveday CE Primary School, Banbury

Trapped

I was stuck. No way of escaping. Suddenly,
something tapped on my shoulder, again and
again. My glasses immediately blurred. I looked
up. I shouted, 'The sky is falling!'
But suddenly, I felt something wet on my arm. It
was just rain, nothing more, nothing less.

Tallulah Gradwell (10)
Bishop Loveday CE Primary School, Banbury

Untitled

One week ago, a family went to the park for a picnic. They had been waiting a week to eat all the sweet and savoury food. The only thing was, when they opened the basket … there was nothing there. The only thing was, was to go to the café.

Eilidh Smith (10)
Bishop Loveday CE Primary School, Banbury

The Big, Ugly, Hairy Monster

I was really worried. It was coming closer, the big, ugly, hairy monster. It was going to rip me to pieces. Down the hall it came. Round the corner. I was sweating. I opened my eyes. There was my dog giving his ball to me to throw again. Silly me!

Natasha Judd (10)
Bishop Loveday CE Primary School, Banbury

Lost

My knees were wobbling. My arms were sweating. I was in a graveyard. I didn't know what to do. I heard a noise. I was really scared. I didn't even know how I got here. Then, I found myself in my bed and then realised it was all a dream.

Sammy Westgate (10)
Bishop Loveday CE Primary School, Banbury

The Terrible Task

I shivered as I crept up the stairs. Sweat dripped off my head. I pushed the door open and there it was. My messy bedroom lay before me. The terrible task of cleaning it seemed impossible.

Charlotte Pearce (9)
Bishop Loveday CE Primary School, Banbury

The Monster

Alex lived near the lake. One night he looked out of his window. He then saw something move in the lake. His body started to sweat. 'It's a big monster!' he screamed. The next day the police told Alex there was no monster. It was a boat. Alex was relieved.

Jack Batters (10)
Bobbing Village School, Sittingbourne

Invasion Of The Daleks

Martha and Jack were getting married. The Doctor went to the wedding. Five minutes later the Daleks came to exterminate the Cybermen. After a fight between them, the Cybermen came. They had a fight. The Daleks won by exterminating them and Martha and Jack had a very happy marriage.

Daniel Ballard (11)
Bobbing Village School, Sittingbourne

Lenny The Lion

Lenny the Lion was singing in the bath. His voice went. He thought it would come back. It didn't! He went to the doctors. The doctor said, 'You sing too much.'
For the next few days, he didn't sing. Suddenly, when he was in the bath, it came back.

Lily Loeber (11)
Bobbing Village School, Sittingbourne

Big Mama

A man called Malcolm was an FBI agent. He had to disguise himself as a woman called Big Mama. He had to be a person looking after kids and keep an eye on their dad. He thought he was doing bad things.
He followed him and caught the bad guy.

Luke Deviell (11)
Bobbing Village School, Sittingbourne

Jimmy Johnson

One day, Jimmy was in America. He had eyes for danger.
'Argh!' somebody screamed.
A sand monster took money from a bank. Jimmy swung in, he kicked him. Jimmy threw water over him. Jimmy hit him. Clumps came off and he was defeated. The job was done once again.

Carl McCann (11)
Bobbing Village School, Sittingbourne

Never Again

Skye had never been so scared. 'I'm never doing this again!' Skye said and screamed as they set off. It was terrifying. To pass the time, Skye thought about what she was going to do. 'I'm glad the plane trip is over!' Skye said when they arrived in Egypt.

Katie Ginn (11)
Bobbing Village School, Sittingbourne

Mum And I

Mum and I went shopping. Then Mum turned round the corner and we crashed. I turned to Mum to see if she was OK. She put her hand on my shoulder. He got away.
After the ambulance, they cleaned us up and came in.

Sarah Reynolds (11)
Bobbing Village School, Sittingbourne

Football Dreams

Tom received the ball. He got past one player. Tom carried on running. Nobody could stop him! Tom came up to a giant! Time stopped … if he scored, they would win! Tom nutmegged the giant. The giant felt humiliated! Tom scored past the keeper! His eyes ascended, what a dream!

Beau Taylor (11)
Bobbing Village School, Sittingbourne

Susan's Stuck

'Help!' cried Susan, 'I'm stuck in a tree!' Susan's dad rushed outside to see what had happened and he realised Susan was hanging from the weakest branch. Next he rang 999 and asked for the Fire Brigade. They arrived in less than two minutes and Susan was safe and sound!

Charlotte Dennis (9)
Bursledon Junior School, Bursledon

Hercules And The Fire

'I see trees on fire,' said Hercules and goes off running to the fire. When he gets there, he sees lots of animals running around scared. He finds a lake and a big, massive bucket. Hercules fills up the bucket and takes it to the fire and puts it out.

Lesley Neale (9)
Bursledon Junior School, Bursledon

Take A Chance

I had nearly won all their money. Sweat trickled down my neck and my shirt stuck to me. One wrong move by them and I'd strip them of everything. But, as I looked on in horror, a policeman arrested me. I love Monopoly, but hate the 'Go To Jail' space!

Jordan Wicks (10)
Bursledon Junior School, Bursledon

71

Midday Mistake

It was a normal lunchtime, like any other, until my friend noticed something gleaming in the sun. At first I didn't see anything. Then I saw a flash of silver. The trees rustled and all was silent. Suddenly, something leapt up in the air. It was a foil sandwich wrapper!

Myfanwy Hack (10)
Bursledon Junior School, Bursledon

Untitled

In a creepy house, on Landmen Lane, inside were bats and scary statues that crept around and jumped at you.
'Boo!'
And if you went in there, they would give you and slug and fly pie. Suddenly, there came a fright!

Hayley Purkiss (10)
Bursledon Junior School, Bursledon

The Best Day Ever!

Today I'm at a very special place. I'm getting a pet. Mum said a gerbil would suit me, but I said, 'I want something a little bigger'.
Dad said a rabbit would be better. Then something caught my eye; a Yorkshire terrier and guess what? Mum said yes! He's mine!

Rachel Humphreys (9)
Bursledon Junior School, Bursledon

Track To School

My feet ache as I track to school. My shoulder gets lower as my bag gets heavier. My mouth gets drier. My hands get colder. I get warmer as the path gets longer. My legs get weaker as I walk further. I reach school. *Ding-dong* goes the bell.

Louise Roberts (10)
Bursledon Junior School, Bursledon

75

My Night-Time Visitor

I got into bed and hid under my covers. The noises started again, like they did the night before, scratching and squeaking, it went on for ages. I crept out of the covers and reached for my torch. As I switched it on it shone onto a tiny little mouse!

Leah Donnarumma (10)
Bursledon Junior School, Bursledon

The Knight And The Dragon

There was once a knight who was paid to protect the kingdom from, well, everything! On one early morning, he was up patrolling the entrance, when a dragon charged at him. He slayed the dragon quickly, with one mighty blow, then showed the head to the king to receive payment.

Christopher Smith (10)
Bursledon Junior School, Bursledon

Trip To The Moon

There once was a spaceman called George. He had been to the moon a few times before, but decided to go again. He got in his NASA rocket and zoomed off into space. He got there and the moon turned to cheese.
'Cheese!' he said.
'Try some, George!'
'Beautifully yummy!'

Ashli Burt (10)
Bursledon Junior School, Bursledon

The Beauty Salon

The salon was deserted, another day of
twiddling my thumbs.
Suddenly, in burst Candy. 'I must have a
makeover! I'm doing a photo-shoot for Vogue!'
Here's my chance to transform her into a
princess. I worked fast, cutting, colouring,
styling and tweaking. Oh! The colour had gone
green … !

Natasha Edwards (10)
Bursledon Junior School, Bursledon

Alien Invite

While Tom was playing, he saw a flying saucer.
Two strange creatures came out and said, 'Do
you want to come to space with us?'
'I would love to! But for how long?' said Tom.
'For the rest of your life.'
'Sorry, I can't go for that long.'
'OK, bye!'

Callum Durnford (10)
Bursledon Junior School, Bursledon

The Lost Space Ship

There was an alien who came from Uranus. He flew down to Earth for fuel. He went and got some fuel, but he forgot where his ship was. He had to ask all the animals if they had seen it anywhere, but nobody saw it.
'There it is!' he cried.

Thomas Sketcher (10)
Bursledon Junior School, Bursledon

A Visitor From Space

Tom, Elizabeth, Ellie and Simon were one
happy family. Simon and Ellie put the children
to bed on a dark, clear night.
'What's that whirring sound?'
Mum rushed in. 'Did you see those lights?'
There was a crash. Little green men escaped
their pod! What a night for all!

Lydia Hallam
Bursledon Junior School, Bursledon

The Alien

I awoke to a tapping noise. It was an alien with a green face and bulgy red eyes. He was playing Space Invaders on my computer. He beat my high score. I hid my face under my covers, then he played Star Wars on my PlayStation. Was I dreaming? Maybe!

Macauley Czak (10)
Bursledon Junior School, Bursledon

Medusa Vs Hercules

Hercules was a fashion king. He wore mirrored sunglasses. How his friends would laugh! Medusa came to town and was turning everyone into stone. That was until she saw her reflection in his sunglasses and that was the end of her!
Hercules said, 'Now everyone will want these glasses!'

Elliot Foulkes (10)
Bursledon Junior School, Bursledon

The Mystery Of The Party

I walked to the Hallowe'en Party. As I opened the door, a shiver crept down my spine. It was empty, no one was there. I clutched hold of my pumpkin bucket. I walked in. 'Hello?' I called. There it was, the skeleton of Alford Winsley. It is true, the legend.

Hollie Fearnley (10)
Bursledon Junior School, Bursledon

Untitled

Hey there! Once upon a time there was a little boy who did not like his family. But this little boy was very special because he had powers, like lightning and thunder. So the little boy said to his mam and dad, 'I want to be a hero for life!'

Cain Simpson (9)
Bursledon Junior School, Bursledon

Rabid Rabbit

A rabbit got into Cindy's garden. She was only three and was excited. She picked him up. He bit her arm. She screamed painfully. Jimmy, her brother, saw Cindy crying. The rabbit kept biting. Jimmy grabbed his stick. 'Run, Cindy!' He raised his stick to strike …
'Morning, Jimmy!' Mum shouted.

Alex Wiltshire (10)
Bursledon Junior School, Bursledon

The Eleventh Doctor

I got sucked into the raw power of time and space (the time vortex). I was alone. Then my body turned to ash. It landed in the 21st century. My ashes rose to the sun. I am the eleventh Doctor. Regenerated once more. My blue eyes, my smooth skin, unrecognisable!

Connaire Webling (10)
Bursledon Junior School, Bursledon

The Monkey And The Croc

Once there lived a hungry croc. He saw a monkey walking by, hid and watched him come closer and then snuck up behind him and with a humungous snap of his mighty jaws, the monkey had gone! The croc thought he was delicious and licked his rather large teeth clean!

Ellie Cunningham (10)
Bursledon Junior School, Bursledon

The Lonely Dragon

Once upon a time, in a land far away, there lived a dragon. The dragon was lonely. He wanted some friends.

One day, when the dragon was walking through the village, he bumped into a boy. The boy hid, but the dragon said, 'Will you be my friend?'

Conor Hatcher (10)
Bursledon Junior School, Bursledon

My Dog's Journey

One day we moved house, 'cause my mum had a job nearby. Suddenly, our dog, Monty, had disappeared! We just knew that he must have gone to our old house. These are the things he passed through; fields, woods and main roads! Then, 'You're there!' Monty returned, fit and healthy.

Katie Turl (9)
Bursledon Junior School, Bursledon

The Lucky Spider

There once was a spider who was running along a tunnel away from a mole.
'I'll get you!' the mole said.
Suddenly, the spider fell down a hole! He fell a long way and then managed to spin a web, which saved him. He was a lucky spider that day!

Liam Heemskerk (10)
Bursledon Junior School, Bursledon

Birthday Wish

One day, a girl called Daisy, had her 10th birthday. When she blew out her candles, she wished she could be a fairy.
The next day, her wish came true! A fairy gave her a special shell, so she could be a fairy any time she liked.
'Thank you!'

Georgia McColl (10)
Bursledon Junior School, Bursledon

A True Story

One night I needed a drink. I went downstairs to get one, but when I opened the door I saw something move! It looked like a rat! So I ran upstairs to tell my mum. We went downstairs and she opened the door and it was my brother's shoe!

Hadyn Cozens (10)
Bursledon Junior School, Bursledon

Dragon's Doom

Darkness fell, a strange whirling wind echoed through the village. As villagers slept, an eerie shadow swept across the roofs of their huts. Gigantic wings blocked the moon's light. In a clearing stood a valiant knight. He stared in horror and drew his sword, thrusting it into the dragon's heart.

Keiran Woods (10)
Bursledon Junior School, Bursledon

Titanic

Everybody wanted to go on its first voyage, because it was said to be unsinkable. It sailed from Southampton full of passengers, but halfway to New York, it sank after hitting an iceberg. Most of the people died. It was the Titanic.

Ben Boyle (10)
Bursledon Junior School, Bursledon

The Caterpillar And The Pheasant Shooters

I was looking for my lunch, when I heard footsteps and gunshots. I knew I would get squashed. I kept still. The noise was incredible! They were getting closer. I held my breath. They passed by. The dog stopped to collect a pheasant. It's quiet again, they have gone.

Carly Bevis (9)
Bursledon Junior School, Bursledon

The Lost Bird

Once upon a time, there was a bird who was flying up high. One day came and something very sad happened. He was flying and got lost. He sat on the ground for days. After that, he saw some friends and lived happily ever after.

Jack Parker (10)
Bursledon Junior School, Bursledon

A Day In The Life Of A Mouse!

One day I was walking along the street, when a big bundle of clothing fell on my head! I couldn't get out! Then the dustbin man came. He looked like a giant to me! Off I went in the red van. Now I'm watching over you in the high heavens!

Ami McCann (10)
Bursledon Junior School, Bursledon

A Human's Nightmare

It glared at me. It was tall, heavy and it fluttered in the air. It would take hours to defeat. It had no arms, no legs and no face, only a body. I was worried, this giant monstrosity - it was growling! I wish I didn't have to mark this homework!

Ben Thorburn (10)
Burstow Primary School, Horley

The Sleepwalker

He was running away from the police when he saw a wall he thought he could jump, but he ran into the wall. He woke up. He was sleepwalking and had ran into his wardrobe. So he got into his lovely bed and went to sleep.

Kieran Hammond (10)
Burstow Primary School, Horley

Win! Win!

I was racing so fast in my Formula One car. *Bang!* Another car had driven straight into me and I was rolling. Suddenly, with a jolt, I remembered I had fallen asleep during a racing game on my Game Boy. I had lost!

James Budgen (11)
Burstow Primary School, Horley

The Big Race

He was leading in the race on the last lap. His arch rival was catching him up. He went over the jump, but then his enemy overtook him. But on the last corner he took the lead and fell off. His brother had beaten him in a bike race.

Joe Maslen (11)
Burstow Primary School, Horley

In The Sea

There I am, playing in the sea, splashing up and down, playing with my rubber duck. But I was only playing in the bath. Then I was told to get out. I thought I was drowning, but I was not.

Zoe Foster (11)
Burstow Primary School, Horley

The Tiger

The tiger jumped out. I ran and ran. Outside I saw something that looked like it had people in it. I ran to it. I looked inside, but it must have been my imagination, because no one was in there. A hand grabbed my shoulder. It was only Mum!

Emily Charman (10)
Burstow Primary School, Horley

Stupid Nuts

He jumped up and saw a big acorn, but suddenly, a big wind blew up on Nuts. He shouted, 'Mother! Mother! Help!'
His mother came and said, 'Where are you, my son?'
'Up here!' called Nuts.
'Oh!' said his mother.
Suddenly, there was fire.
'Wake up! It's time for school!'

Casey Knaggs (7)
Burstow Primary School, Horley

Flying

I'm flying, flying up in the sky to go see my family on the other side of the world. Going past clouds, over mountains, islands, seeing amazing things I've never seen before. I'm finally there. The plane rumbles and tumbles along the runway, where I'm in Australia to visit family.

Lauran White (9)
Burstow Primary School, Horley

The Jumper

I was riding my amazing horse, galloping through the field. I was riding Puzzle, the best jumper at the stable, when Puzzle stopped. He had seen Blue, another horse. She was about to jump. Puzzle picked up speed and jumped over. I screamed, I had fallen off my bike!

Emily Ashby (11)
Burstow Primary School, Horley

The Race

At last I have taken the lead over Valentino Rossi and Casey Stoner. I'm going into the last lap. I'm lapping everyone. Still I race on. I turn the final corner onto the home straight. I have won!

Smack! I have fallen off my bicycle in my back garden!

Danny Knaggs (11)
Burstow Primary School, Horley

The War

I'm in the war of the lands. I was sent to the
forest to fight the goblins. There are zombies
with axes as well. We are winning. I just killed
a goblin. I'm deep in the forest now. Men
everywhere and goblins too.
I am daydreaming, hitting trees.

Alex Winterburn (11)
Burstow Primary School, Horley

The Big Mountain

I was climbing a very tall mountain. I was almost at the top. It felt great. The first person to ever get to the top. The wind in your face, ah! I loved it! But suddenly, my leg got caught in the playground ropes and I was hanging upside down.

Mark Strong (10)
Burstow Primary School, Horley

Computer Game

I'm in the Second World War and my side is losing. I run down the barricades, towards the enemy. I'm low on health and could faint any minute now. Bother! I've been hit and it's game over! It was just a game level I can't get past, because it's hard.

Oliver Rushby (9)
Burstow Primary School, Horley

The Smelly Monster

I was as quiet as a mouse. The monster was getting closer and closer to the door. The beast opened the door and a bad smell crept in. The beast quietly tiptoed up to me. It picked up a pillow and sneaked up my ladder.
Ouch! My brother hit me.

Cameron Lamond (11)
Burstow Primary School, Horley

The Racer

I was speeding down the track, heart pounding, the wind blowing my hair. I overtook another car round a sharp corner. I'm winning! My heart was still pounding with one lap to go. I went round the last bend, skidding, spun round and fell off my bike!

Leyna Salter (11)
Burstow Primary School, Horley

My Favourite Dream

I was flying. I was as high as a bird. Oh no! I was falling! *Boing!* I was saved by the trampoline again. This time I was actually flying. I was flying over my next door's fence. Oh no! *Bang! Crash!*

Sam Austen (11)
Burstow Primary School, Horley

115

The Prince

Long ago, a prince slayed monsters. When he crept into a cave, he found himself surrounded by monsters. In a flash of lightning, he pulled out his sword and said, 'Super duper luper slayer!' The monsters fell to the ground. The prince summoned his sleigh and loaded the monsters on.

Martin Atfield (11)
Burstow Primary School, Horley

The Princess' Party

Once, there was a princess called Rebecca.
She was unpopular. She did not have a prince
and she was single for some time.
Then it was her birthday and everyone heard
the music and followed it to her castle and
became her friend.

Alice Dunstan (7)
Burstow Primary School, Horley

The Crisp

A boy was eating a packet of crisps, when he heard a voice. The crisp was running away! The boy chased the crisp and caught it.
'Oi! Get off me!'
The crisp jumped and got run over by a Walkers Crisp truck and it stopped. The driver held a funeral.

Daniel Apps (10)
Burstow Primary School, Horley

Changing

He walked into the light of the moon in the forest. The boy shivered, wishing he'd brought a coat. Weirdly he began scratching rapidly, on his arms and face. His arms were now 'danger' red and sore. He saw repulsive, thick brown hair growing on him. He was a werewolf!

Emily Jones (11)
Burstow Primary School, Horley

The Gerbera Fairy

She sat on the petal of a gerbera, her hair flowing past her waist, as she sang the gerbera song. 'La, la! says the gerbera in beautiful lime green …'
She stopped as a muddy hand seized her, but put her down again.
'Sorry, hope you didn't get wet!'

Dana Chucki (11)
Burstow Primary School, Horley

The Monster

I was walking down the road from getting some Cola, when suddenly, a green bogie-like monster jumped out.

Shame, it was my geography teacher who came round for tea. When we ate, there was a ghost dropping his food everywhere. At last he went home in a taxi.

Matthew Brown (10)
Burstow Primary School, Horley

The Wendy House Island

I was strolling on the beautiful island. It was a fantastic view! It was great. I was staying in a hotel made out of diamonds, but suddenly I heard, 'Tea time!' and I found myself in the wendy house in the garden.

'Ow!'

I hit my head.

George Dunstan (9)
Burstow Primary School, Horley

Mount Everest Disaster

I was climbing Mount Everest with the wind
pulling me back, making my hair stand on end.
I could faintly see the top, when suddenly a
rock I was holding onto fell.
'Whoops! Argh!' I had fallen off the climbing wall
and was abseiling to the floor.

Emma Bradley (10)
Burstow Primary School, Horley

Ripper And His Long But Short Adventure

Ripper jumped over the dreaded River of Death, punched a lion on the nose, got chased by a monkey, until he got bored, then chopped off its head. Stopped for lunch near a nice river, got up, killed the dragon, ran up the stairs to find the
princess … was gone!

Harry Timperley (10)
Carlton Hill Primary School, Brighton

The Washing Up

The brown gravy-like goo stared at me, daring me to pull out a prize. Who knows what, stirred under the mucky brown liquid? I plunged my hand in and pulled out an unlucky prize. Lifting up a rough yellow and green monster, to wipe across my unlucky prize.

Rubie Rowsell (11)
Carlton Hill Primary School, Brighton

The Terrifying Monster Stopper

Jamal was playing a game and he needed one more level. Jamal was so happy, then … he went to the next level. He said, 'Yes!' Jamal started to play his best at the last level of the game. The game suddenly stopped. It must have been a virus.

Richard Mensah (10)
Carlton Hill Primary School, Brighton

The Snail

The snail wanted to go somewhere else, so he crossed the most busy road in the world and dodged a million cars. He lost an eye. He was very hungry, so he crossed faster. He got to the curb and ate for a while, then got trodden on.

Cameron Beach (11)
Carlton Hill Primary School, Brighton

The Tear-Shaped Avocado

I was at school sitting at a table, when suddenly a 3D teardrop landed on my lap. It was all curvy and bumpy, hard and rough. I closed my eyes and imagined I was on a basketball court and threw it for three points.
'Who threw that avocado?'

Abby Lockwood (10)
Carlton Hill Primary School, Brighton

The Game

Walking up the long walkway as the waving choppers clap against each other. As the round, white planet is placed on the centre of the battlefield. *'Kick'* I ran across the warzone, searching for freedom. The high-flying planet drifted over the tall standing warriors blocking the netted cage. Goal!

Tariq Bushara (11)
Carlton Hill Primary School, Brighton

The Eraser

It just had to go. It was ruining the land under him. The white enemy came closer to him. Will he ever be the same again? It was going by the millimetre. Then it was gone.
'Have you finished rubbing out that stickman?' yelled Jane.

Andrew Hackett (10)
Carlton Hill Primary School, Brighton

The Relaxing Tube

Abbie entered the dull room. She was shaking like a leaf as she approached the tube. Abbie stepped in and slipped under the clear liquid. Out of the blue, Abbie gave an almighty yell, *'Argh!'* After a long rest, Abbie stepped out. 'Have you finished in the bath?' shouted Mum.

Natasha Pollard (10)
Carlton Hill Primary School, Brighton

The Big, Round Monster

All I could see was a fat, round monster, with glistening white crystal on top of its surface. I looked at him, he looked at me. I put him in my mouth. His blood exploded and squirted on my new jumper.

'Have you finished your jam doughnut yet?' questioned Mum.

Gabrielly Ramos (11)
Carlton Hill Primary School, Brighton

The Mirror

Sitting, staring into the mirror, all I could see was a knotty monster staring back. So I picked up the spiky base that was on my desk. I tried to fight the monster. He got worn out, but it was still there.

Mum called, 'Have you finished brushing your hair?'

Nicole Dutschke (9)
Carlton Hill Primary School, Brighton

The Red Monster

All I could see was a heart-shaped monster staring at me. I sliced its green hair off. I picked it up and placed it on my lip. Screaming, it jumped in. I had to bite and its blood ran down my lip.
'Have you finished your strawberry yet, Leah?'

Chloe Blake (11)
Carlton Hill Primary School, Brighton

The Waterslide

The hard surface of the steep hill tells me it'll be my death. If the hill doesn't take me, the water will. Which way to go? The quick way or the hard way? I can't choose, I'll just run! 'Hurry up, David! It's raining! Go down the slide!'

Arthur Reynolds (10)
Carlton Hill Primary School, Brighton

The Crazy Shower

All the water was pouring down my face. Slimy
goo dripped down my head. After finishing with
the waterfall, I saw slimy liquid dripping down
the side of my face.
'Hurry up, Sara! I want one after you!'
'Do you want me to leave the shower on for
you?'

Geneva Berry (10)
Carlton Hill Primary School, Brighton

The Mystery Tube

Bethany entered the bright, colourful room. She was shaking as she walked towards the tube. She slammed the door behind her. She nervously dipped her foot inside, then she gave a mighty yelp. *'Argh!'* She rushed out of the tube.

'Hurry up in the bath, Bethany!' called Mum.

Terrianne Goodwin (11)
Carlton Hill Primary School, Brighton

The Cheese Monster

The cheese monster was pulled out from under the staircase. The brightness turned into brown mud. My nose blocked with fright. The cheesy waft stunk out the house. The brown, gooey mud ruined the scent. The gas invaded my nose.

'Have you got your shoes on, Ashley?' said Mum.

Louise Flowers (10)
Carlton Hill Primary School, Brighton

The Crazy Animal

It roared. You could hear its footsteps coming through the cave. What could it be? Closer and closer it came. A shiver ran through my body. It roared again. I went to run back, but I couldn't. it was a cliff. What could I do? Think, Jamie, think! *'Raaar!'*

Meghan Burtenshaw (11)
Carlton Hill Primary School, Brighton

The Unicorn

Once upon a time, there lived a princess called Liona. She loved picking flowers. One day, a dragon came and stayed. Then Liona sang sad songs. A unicorn heard the songs and danced around the garden. The dragon danced and then he sneezed and vanished.

Sara Khan (9)
Copthorne Preparatory School, Copthorne

The Falling Egg

Long ago, there was a brave boy called Peter. One day, it was raining and something fell quickly down in the rain. Peter caught it and to his surprise, it was an egg. It was half cracked and he looked in it and saw red burning eyes.

Sarena Bhargava (8)
Copthorne Preparatory School, Copthorne

The Lonely Owl

Once upon a time, there lived a lonely owl. His name was Fluffy. Fluffy didn't have any friends. They didn't like Fluffy because he was so small. Once, when Fluffy went on a walk, he met an owl called Tiny. They became new friends.

Imogen Simmonds (8)
Copthorne Preparatory School, Copthorne

The Killer Shrimp

On a sandy beach, there lived a killer shrimp.
One day, the killer shrimp jumped off his
rock and pinched a child. The child fell to the
ground, dead. Nobody knew how the killer
shrimp had killed the child. The shrimp's secret
was a poisonous pinch.

Ryan Singleton (8)
Copthorne Preparatory School, Copthorne

The Mirror

There was a funny boy called Max. For his birthday he got a mirror. When he looked in the mirror, something was pulling him in. He struggled to get out. He pushed, he pulled, then he was safely out. He made a big mess. He heard his mum coming.

Maya Roberts (8)
Copthorne Preparatory School, Copthorne

The Ancient Horror

We have been stranded in Egypt for a year.
Right now, me and my sister, Rebecca and my
brother, Yoshi, are at the sphinx. Guess what?
We have just found the hidden tomb of Nefertiti
and her child, Cleopatra. I pulled open the door
and Cleopatra glared at me.

Gurdip Ahluwalia (8)
Copthorne Preparatory School, Copthorne

The Rattling Bush

Once, there was a little boy called Bob. He was very clever and his best friend was Ross. They went and played a game in the garden. Then something shook in the bush. What is it? The boys wondered. It was smelly, white and black.

Nia Thomas (8)
Copthorne Preparatory School, Copthorne

Red Eyes

There once was an alien called Red Eyes. He killed anyone in his way. One day, he came to Earth and killed them all. There were only some people left. He set light to the country and ran away.

Nils Kerneis (8)
Copthorne Preparatory School, Copthorne

The Brownie

Once upon a time, there was a boy who couldn't stop laughing. Then a wee man who knew what to do, gave him some brownies. *Puff!* He was gone!

Ross Knight (8)
Copthorne Preparatory School, Copthorne

The Amazed Diver

One day, a diver went 200 metres down and saw a huge octopus spinning slowly in the hot water. The diver took a photograph, when suddenly, the octopus sprayed ink on him. The diver was terrified. He could only stay underwater for 20 seconds.

James Parkin (8)
Copthorne Preparatory School, Copthorne

A Fiery Lie

My friend Jack came over today. He smokes!
He offered me a cigarette in my bedroom. I
didn't approve. Jack accidentally dropped a lit
cigarette. 'Doesn't matter,' he muttered.
Later, Mum asked, 'Was Jack smoking?'
'No!' I lied.
Suddenly, flames burst through my bedroom
door, licking the oak wood frame.

James Hastings (10)
Great Rollright Primary School, Chipping Norton

Granny's House

I wouldn't get out of the car. The boring old cottage was in sight. I was nowhere near my friends. I was visiting my granny's house. I had to sit quietly and play boring board games. The car stopped. Granny opened the door in her best suit of armour.

Lawrence Beck (10)
Great Rollright Primary School, Chipping Norton

Lost

I stumbled around, lost in darkness. It was eight o'clock at night, but it felt like midnight. Normally, Oxford was still bustling with cars and people wandering about. I walked up the main street. *Crash!* I had fallen into one of the hidden traps in the forbidden forest.

Annabelle Fowler (9)
Great Rollright Primary School, Chipping Norton

Jumping

I got on it, into the arena, round, round.
Suddenly, I was in the air, up, up, then down,
down, *thump!*
'Well done, Hannah,' said Alex, my riding
instructor.
I patted my horse Midnight. 'Well, done to you
too,' I whispered to him.

Hannah Keene (10)
Great Rollright Primary School, Chipping Norton

My First Day At School

Alice had a red jacket as she arrived inside the school gate. There were lots of children playing.
'Hey, what's your name?'
'Alice,' said Alice.
Ding-ding! Went the school bell.
'This is Alice, she is new. We will all make you feel welcome here.'
'Yes!' called the class.

Jessica Rose (9)
Great Rollright Primary School, Chipping Norton

My Dog

My dog's name is Bubbles. His grey hair flaps
in the wind. His tail wags.
Two years later: I'm crying, 'Bubble's gone!'
Twenty years later: I'm clearing my cupboards.
'Bubbles, there you are!'
My childhood memories come flooding back. I
think to myself, *wish he wasn't a puppet!*

Lana Sumners (9)
Great Rollright Primary School, Chipping Norton

Disaster Zone

I opened the creaking door. It slammed shut. I was in the room. My heart pounded as I breathed into my gas mask. I snapped my rubber gloves on, picked up some of last month's socks, selected an air freshener from my weapon belt. Finally, my bedroom's back to normal.

Sophie Napier (11)
Great Rollright Primary School, Chipping Norton

Escalators

Grocery shopping is a pain. It just always has to rain. I hate it. Tall, grey and scary monsters gobbling me up. I step on the bottom step, up, up, up. *Argh!* I'm falling, down, down! Oh no! I wish I didn't have a fear of escalators. I'm doomed!

Hannah Blencowe (10)
Great Rollright Primary School, Chipping Norton

The Big Drop

There it was. I thought they were only true in fairy tales. The mighty Cyclops was bearing down on me. I stared into its bloodshot eye. Suddenly, I found myself falling and falling. I awoke to find myself falling. I looked down. I was horrified by what I saw. *Argh!*

Simon Dawson (10)
Great Rollright Primary School, Chipping Norton

The School Lunch

The food smelt horrible today. Old lamb curry.
We sat down and began. It was awful! I couldn't
wait for pudding. Treacle sponge with custard.
It was lovely! We finished, we said Grace, we
were let out to break, table by table. Well, we
still have spaghetti Bolognaise tomorrow.

Tristan Sheppard (12)
Haslemere Preparatory School, Haslemere

Old House

We were walking to the old house, which we play in. when we got to the door, the door flew open. There was an old lady at the door. She shouted at us. We ran up the lane to go home. The lady was at the door.
I woke up.

Ben Poulsom (12)
Haslemere Preparatory School, Haslemere

A Summary Of The Jungle Book

Found by the panther, Bagheera, the man-cub Mowgli was raised by wolves. When Sherekhan the tiger returned to the jungle, Mowgli was in danger. Bagheera took him through the jungle, past dangers of Kaa the snake and King Louie the monkey who wanted him. Mowgli found the man-village.

William Grassick (12)
Haslemere Preparatory School, Haslemere

The Airport

As I got in the car to go to the airport, I started to feel excited. I had waited all year for this holiday. Last year I didn't get a holiday. It was a night flight and it was dark. When we got to the desk, our flight was cancelled.

Eddy Aston (12)
Haslemere Preparatory School, Haslemere

The Bombing

The bombs fell and the city was alight. People ran for cover. Houses exploded and they fell to the ground. I ran down my normally peaceful street. My friend's house was gone and I expect he was too. The bomb shelter was in sight. Only twenty yards. I got there!

Toby Ward (13)
Haslemere Preparatory School, Haslemere

Little Red Riding Hood

Little Red Riding Hood was asked to take food to her grandmother. When she got there, the wolf was in her grandmother's bed. The wolf was about to eat her, when the woodchopper came and killed the wolf and set her grandmother free, from the big, bad, ugly wolf.

Tom Lowndes (13)
Haslemere Preparatory School, Haslemere

The Party

One happy, pretty summer's morning, I went for a quick bike ride. On the way I saw a dog on its own. I cycled on, stopped off at the park. I saw dogs arriving. Eventually there were 50 dogs. They turned up the music, got on their hind legs and danced.

Ross Power (13)
Haslemere Preparatory School, Haslemere

In Town

I was walking into town and everyone was running and screaming, going in the opposite direction to me. It was as if there was a gunman up the road. It was so frantic, that it started to freak me out. To my utter surprise, it was a gunman!

Colum Jordan (13)
Haslemere Preparatory School, Haslemere

The Rogue

There was a boy. An impish boy. This boy was going to impress his girlfriend by sneaking into school. This boy had with him three spray cans. Blue, green and red. On the gym wall, he spray-painted 'School Sucks!'
The headmistress walked up. 'I think expulsion, Mr Walker!'

Freddie Thomas (12)
Haslemere Preparatory School, Haslemere

167

Hobo

I was lying on the floor. I have been in the spot for twenty years, always half-drunk. A man was passing by. 'Got any spare change,' I mumbled. The man just spat in my face and kept walking. Out of every three people, one would hurt me. Life sucks!

Dylan Surrey Robertson (13)
Haslemere Preparatory School, Haslemere

The Inferno

The incredible flame shot up into the air. I watched it evolve, slowly becoming bigger and bigger, until the minute flame, at first, turned into a colossal inferno. I stumbled back in awe, shocked at what I saw. Suddenly, a sharp spark flew out and caught fire on my trousers.

Johnny Taylor (13)
Haslemere Preparatory School, Haslemere

My First Time At The Pub

I arrived at the pub with a couple friends in a Clio. We walked toward the counter. After a minute, the pints were put on the table. *'Ahh!'* I said. After that, more came. I woke up with a headache. 'Never again,' I said to myself.

William McKinnon (13)
Haslemere Preparatory School, Haslemere

My New Job

I walked up to the old door. As I knocked, I could hear someone telling off a small child. All of a sudden, there was a smack, followed by a bloodcurdling scream. Suddenly, I didn't want the job anymore. I considered running, but my feet were glued to the ground.

Zoe Whipp (10)
Kingswood Primary School, Tadworth

Fantasy Football

Nails were being bitten to the bone, as Beckham lined the free-kick up. It was the World Cup Final and England were playing Brazil. Beckham took one more glance at the score, 0-0, with a minute left, the ref blew his whistle and up stepped Beckham. *Goal!* England win!

Dean Wilson (10)
Kingswood Primary School, Tadworth

Getting Up

The shouting was coming from downstairs. I heard some thuds getting louder and louder. The door opened with a creak. Something came through the door. My mum. She took one step, she gave a sigh, 'Will you *please* get up, Jim Bob!'

Matthew Maycock (9)
Kingswood Primary School, Tadworth

In Trouble

My legs were trembling in my brand new trousers. I couldn't move. I knew it was behind me. It was the evil monster. I couldn't turn my head. I was going to cry. My teeth were chattering, so my chewing gum fell onto the floor. It was the evil headmaster.

Scarlett McNamara (10)
Kingswood Primary School, Tadworth

Home Alone

I got back from school. I went into my house.
'Mum! Dad!' I yelled. They weren't home yet.
It was getting dark. I went to sit down. I was
trembling like mad. I heard a gunshot. I quickly
got up. I saw a stranger, dead on the cold floor.

Holly Stevenson (10)
Kingswood Primary School, Tadworth

Untitled

My ears popped as we started to land. The plane made a sudden jerk. I was flung to the other side of the plane, banging my head on the wall. *'Ouch!'* I yelled and fell on the floor. 'Damn it!' the plane hit the runway at top speed. 'At last!'

Daniel Serne (10)
Kingswood Primary School, Tadworth

Dark Forest

It was called Dark Forest. He was walking, trying to find a shelter to live in. When he found a tree, he lay under it. He stared at the tree. It moved. It had eyes. He ran for his life, but did he make it out alive?
No one knows.

Callum Barker (10)
Kingswood Primary School, Tadworth

Bart's Incident

Bart was doing his usual thing, annoying his sister. She was good at dodging. That minute, Marge came in and stood in front of Bart. Lisa grabbed a saucer and did a Frisbee throw and cut a big chunk of Marge's hair off and knocked Bart on the noggin.

'Bart!'

Jessica Jackson (10)
Langton Green Primary School, Tunbridge Wells

What Cars Can Really Do To You

'What?' I looked around (in my dream). I was in a car park. Suddenly, all the trees melted, the cars and the people melted. I gazed at my melting hands, the night sky … in a flash of bright lights, I woke up. A bright car loomed over my dead body.

Benjamin Sainsbury (10)
Langton Green Primary School, Tunbridge Wells

Dino Run

Silently, she crept through the leaves and peered through a hole in the branches. There it was, a T-rex. Suddenly, Lily fell loudly. The T-rex looked up and unfortunately saw her. She zoomed through the trees, the ghastly beast following her. It was so close now, it … then she awoke.

Olivia McDaid (10)
Langton Green Primary School, Tunbridge Wells

Piece Of Cake

'There's been a robbery at the cottage.'
'What's missing?'
The old lady ushers the constable into the
scullery.
'Two eggs, milk from the jug, flour from the
pantry, sugar and a bag of dried fruit.'
As they sat dumbfounded at the table, the old
lady asks, 'Slice of cake?'

Sylvia Villa (10)
Langton Green Primary School, Tunbridge Wells

Monster's Ink

Olivia was hiding. Suddenly, she shuddered, everything was cold. She felt it shuffle and huffle about. Then she heard a *drip-drop, drip-drop.* She could see the monster's ink on the floor. It was a murky swamp colour. Just then ... 'Olivia! your tea's spilt on the floor, silly girl!'

Olivia Clarke (9)
Langton Green Primary School, Tunbridge Wells

Potato Heads

Gingerly I crept into my science lab. Had my cloning experiment worked? It had. I had just become the first person to clone … a potato! Suddenly, both potatoes grew legs and started dancing around the science lab. How amazing! I had just created a whole new race of living creatures.

Timothy Knapp (10)
Langton Green Primary School, Tunbridge Wells

The Solitary Silhouette

Eventually, Nelly closed her weary eyes. She dreamt of repulsive monsters, bloodthirsty dragons that could burst your eardrums with their bloodcurdling roar!
Suddenly, Nelly woke with a start. She gazed around, caught sight of a silhouette. Nelly gingerly switched her light on. It was only her teddy bear!

Rowena Liley (10)
Langton Green Primary School, Tunbridge Wells

Cinderella

At the ball, Cinderella would have danced all
night, but her second-hand phone rang.
'Hello dear! forgot to tell you. You …'
But too late, the already crackled-up voice
disappeared.
'My phone ran out,' sighed Cindy.
Bong! rang the bell in the tower and Cindy
found herself in rags!

Lizzie Avis (10)
Langton Green Primary School, Tunbridge Wells

Paper People

Once, there was a world, where drawings came to life. Every night, they would venture out of their world and absorb humans and take them back to the world of paper! Where they would regurgitate them as paper people and make them slaves to help make a new *paper* race!

Oliver Tomlinson (10)
Langton Green Primary School, Tunbridge Wells

The Bad Day

I've been kidnapped. I am a child. I've been locked in a dirty and deserted cellar. There's no way out. I can hear people screaming and shouting. I'm done for. It sounds like they're dying up there. I've got to get out now. I can hear someone coming. *Argh!*

Josh Gentry (10)
Langton Green Primary School, Tunbridge Wells

187

The Mystery Cat

Creeping quietly, we raided a shack. We spotted a cat. It walked a little, then waited. It wanted us to follow.

'I think we should,' whispered Mary.

The cat led us to the dump. It clawed at a heap of rubbish. I realised it wanted the tin of can nibbles.

Sophie Tang (10)
Langton Green Primary School, Tunbridge Wells

Too ... The Wrong Planet

Amazingly, something flew down and landed uneasily in the park. The large door opened and a miniature green thing strolled out. It murmured something like, 'Are we at Mars yet?'
'Nope, we're on Earth,' said a gigantic blue thing.
'Doh! I'm no good at flying,' explained the miniature green thing.

Joe Peck (10)
Langton Green Primary School, Tunbridge Wells

The Big Bang!

Loudly a wee, fluorescent alien stamped along the freezing planet Pluto, after an argument with his dad about a game they could play at the barbecue tonight.

Suddenly, a bomb came flying into the planet.

'Hey, can we play pass the bomb tonight?'

'Yes!'

Kaboom! Now they're off to Heaven.

Jamie Weller (10)
Langton Green Primary School, Tunbridge Wells

The Black Figure!

A girl emerged from the mist. She peered through the darkness. Nothing was to be seen. Suddenly, a black figure was mysteriously coming towards her. She panicked. She felt the figure's horrible cold hands around her neck. He strangled her to death and nothing was heard of that poor girl.

Madeleine Gallivan (11)
Laverock School, Oxted

A Mountain Encounter

I started my trek to Mount Everest, shaking with cold. Slowly, I made my way up to the peak, with frostbitten fingers. At last! I had reached the top.

'Emma!' shouted Lucy, 'Time to go home!'

My mountain vanished. The top of the climbing frame was all that was left.

Emma-Jane Gordon (11)
Laverock School, Oxted

Embarrassment

I waited excitedly behind the big, brown curtains on the stage, with my friend, Milly. We couldn't wait any longer, so we started putting our legs straight up in the air, playing about. Suddenly, the scary headteacher looked spookily behind the curtains and saw us. We were so embarrassed.

Hannah Kent (11)
Laverock School, Oxted

The Magical Land

I jumped out of bed. I thought I was having a nightmare. My heart was beating out of my skin. I could hear voices coming from the cellar. I crept downstairs and opened the cellar door. It creaked loudly and I could see a magical land in front of me.

Rosha Henley (11)
Laverock School, Oxted

The Door Of Doom

Zoe edged closer to the door. She gripped the handle tightly, wobbled it rapidly and charged it down. The wood splintered into pieces. Zoe entered the house. The floor creaked beneath her. The shadows loomed above her. Suddenly, ghostly white hands gripped her round the neck. She sank into unconsciousness.

Jessica Siddell (11)
Laverock School, Oxted

Barnaby

I crept into the forest, my shadow tickling
my back. Four thick claws gripped my leg!
A werewolf? A tiger? No, Barnaby! So that's
where my kitten was!

Jemma Davies (11)
Laverock School, Oxted

The Ride Of A Lifetime

I was dragged onto the roller coaster. It gradually picked up speed, going up and up. A heart-stopping feeling emerged from inside me. Suddenly, it was silent, I couldn't breathe. A chill ran down my spine. Then, down we went, screaming. A sudden stop told me it was over.

Theola Sturridge (11)
Laverock School, Oxted

The Scare

Splash! I dive into the cool Hawaiian waters. The water shimmers all around me. The coral on the seabed holds lots of life. Oh no! here comes a great white shark! Get me out of the water!
Wow! That was the best holiday ever!

Sophie Belchambers (11)
Laverock School, Oxted

The Monsters!

She ran as fast as she could. She couldn't face the horror of seeing the monsters again. Then she looked, but then she tripped and fell. She turned around. She was trembling all over. Then, she saw her two best friends in Hallowe'en costumes. She had forgotten it was Hallowe'en!

Romany Colligon (11)
Laverock School, Oxted

The Blood-Red Beast

My knees were trembling as I took a step forward. It was my turn. The monster grabbed me and set off. Twisting and turning, the nasty beast chucked me left and right. I screamed very loudly. Just then, it slowed down. Dizzily I stepped off the bright red roller coaster.

Zoe Carver (11)
Laverock School, Oxted

Attack Of The Pebble Monster

One day, a warrior named Henry went down to the depths of the underworld to save his wife. However, Hades knew of his plan. So he sent out a pebble monster to destroy him. Henry was not expecting a monster. Unfortunately Henry was decapitated. Poor Henry never stood a chance.

Michael Tubbs (11)
Medina Primary School, Portsmouth

John And The Minotaur

In the temple, a man called John had been sentenced to a job on the forbidden island. So, John grabbed his boat and drifted off. On the way, it started to thunder and lightning and he got there, but as soon as he got on, there was a Minotaur (dead).

Ryan Martin (11)
Medina Primary School, Portsmouth

The Thing!

My eyes glued, my heart shattered, there it was, a thing. What could it be? Just then, it stared back, the face of my nightmare. I attempted to hide, but my shadow showed it all. Suddenly, the decrepit beast chased me with its claws of rage. It struck me.

Danielle Scott (11)
Medina Primary School, Portsmouth

The Missing Girl

One sunny day, a Greek meeting took place in an ancient temple. Outside the temple was a Minotaur, hiding behind some flowering bushes. As a young girl came to pick some flowers, she came over. The Minotaur grabbed her. The girl was never to be seen again. Or was she?

Georgia Harriss (11)
Medina Primary School, Portsmouth

The Beast You Never Escape

In the murkiest and most funereal place in the history of ancient Greece, embarked the most formidable creature ever to walk amongst the world. Many intimidated explorers entered, however, they never stumbled out.
Is it me? I'm in the cave. I flip back into the wrath of total darkness demised.

Kyle Ridout (11)
Medina Primary School, Portsmouth

205

No More Men

'Dead, dead, dead,' the annoyed guard
mumbled, 'all of the elites are dead.'
The guard stabbed the wall with fury.
'W-well what shall we do?' stuttered the slave
anxiously.
'We'll have to get some more.'
They searched all the town. No men. What were
they to do? Die? Die!

Harrison Smith (11)
Medina Primary School, Portsmouth

The Night Before Dawn

As the temple crumbled, still Pebble sat there. He had done wrong, but he wanted to punish himself in a cruel, harmful way. If only we had time, we tried and tried, but he was gone. From that day on, nobody dared to go near the old ruins!

Deanna King (10)
Medina Primary School, Portsmouth

The Boy And The Temple

One morning, a scared, but always happy little boy ran into an old Greek temple. Out of light and into darkness, the boy was shaking as he walked past and the candles lit themselves. A voice came from up ahead.

'Ahh!'

Like a bolt, he ran.

Eloise Tribble (10)
Medina Primary School, Portsmouth

The Highway To Hell

One day, a three-headed dog called Cerberus, started terrorising Greece, by eating all the humans that lived there. A few weeks later, nearly all the humans had died, except the navy. One evening, Cerberus came to the beach and glared at the huge ships, then they shot him dead.

Henry Barker (11)
Medina Primary School, Portsmouth

The Smoke Of Darkness

Staring, staring, straight at me, was the ferocious Minotaur. The beast with the bloodthirsty teeth, sharp eyes and sharpened horns. My legs shaking, with the weapon in my hand. I struck the beast, but it was too strong. I struck it again and again. Finally, the beast tumbled to the floor.

James Bailey (11)
Medina Primary School, Portsmouth

The Dungeon Of Death

I was alone, all alone, or so I thought. Quietly I searched for a way out of this dungeon (this nightmare). Suddenly, I heard a raging roar. Just then, a thing ran at me, like a lion hunting its prey. I stood dead in my tracks. Death had taken me!

Rosie Graham (11)
Medina Primary School, Portsmouth

Disaster!

I heard screams from the temple. It was funny, because it was a peaceful place. So, I rushed in as fast as my legs could carry me. To my surprise, it was a Minotaur - bulging muscles, head of a bull and body of a man. My heart spelt disaster. *Disaster!*

Dominic Vaughan (10)
Medina Primary School, Portsmouth

Fly

Carefully, Chloe stared at all the numbers on the seats, when finally she saw the number twenty-two. Cautiously, she shifted her suitcase in the top cupboard and her laptop. Then she cuddled up to the side of the plane, but yet again, she had cuddled up to the wrong seat.

Sophie Barrie (9)
St Swithun's Catholic Primary School, Portsmouth

A Hawaiian Holiday

Strolling smoothly along the gleaming white sands of Hawaii, also looking out along the shimmering blue horizon, I sat down on the sandy beach and started to build a small, towered sandcastle, with a touch of water added to make it secure. Suddenly I turned my body. Water surrounded me!

Natalie Gorman (11)
St Swithun's Catholic Primary School, Portsmouth

Spider Flurry

Professor Ben was doing an experiment on spider venom. He had four spiders which were poisonous, in a large box. He took out one of them. They were fluffy, cold. Suddenly, the one that was in the palm of his hand, lashed out and bit him. He froze. He'd died.

Michael Olive (10)
St Swithun's Catholic Primary School, Portsmouth

Glob Trob

Emma and Hannah were walking to school.
They were the only people there!
'What's going on?'
'Let's go and see!'
They found an ugly little alien.
'Hello!'
'Glob trob!'
'Who are you?'
'Glob trob!'
'Is that it?'
'Yes!'
'Great, now it has a sense of humour!'
Hiss! They were vaporised.

Hannah Haughey (9)
St Swithun's Catholic Primary School, Portsmouth

Kleeba Gleeba Treeba
Or The Alien

'I saw an alien!'
'No you didn't!'
'I did!'
'Where?'
'Come on, I'll show you.'
They walked for two hours. Finally they found it.
Green with yellow spots. Small blue horns. Red
eyes.
'Gleeba fleeba treeba!'
'Wow!' said Kate
'Wow!' said Jim
'Kleeba treeba,' said the alien.
Then … *poof!* Gone!

Sara Weston (10)
St Swithun's Catholic Primary School, Portsmouth

217

Big Bang

A witch was explaining to her child, if spells go right, it goes *whiz, pop, bang!* Big witch had nearly perfected eternal life, so that night, little witch put a whiz popper into the cauldron, then lit some dynamite. *Bang!*
'Oops!' said the little witch, 'It went a bit wrong!'

Lauren Nicholls & Emma Ford (10)
St Swithun's Catholic Primary School, Portsmouth

Golden Coin

A small, green fairy was looking for her mum's golden coin. She looked in the shop. There it was! She grabbed it in a rush and gave it to her mum.
'Wow! So many, I only lost one!'
She bit it.
'This is chocolate!
I asked for a golden coin!'

Zsofia Pap (11)
St Swithun's Catholic Primary School, Portsmouth

Empty Village

I looked. No one. 'Hello? Hello?' No answer. I was shocked. I couldn't even hear a whisper. I thought it was crazy. I had a warm feeling but I was very excited. I didn't understand, it was too quiet. Yesterday it was full, today it's a very empty village.

Sophie Dearing & Mary McMillan (10)
St Swithun's Catholic Primary School, Portsmouth

Candy

Candy was a little girl. She was ten. She had a dad named Caramel and a mum called Cherry. One sunny day, Candy went to school. She made three friends called Toffee, Fudge and Jellytot. They went shopping with each other and spent money. They became the best of friends!

Lara Domaszewska (9)
St Swithun's Catholic Primary School, Portsmouth

221

Thunder Forest

Lightning crashed down on Thunder Forest.
Lillie had given up on picking the berries she
was supposed to pick. Sticky, boiling mud
had got all over her eyes. She couldn't see
anything. Crawling into a ditch, finally she had
somewhere to rest!

'Argh!' A tree was crashing down on hear …

Nicola Flynn (9)
St Swithun's Catholic Primary School, Portsmouth

Untitled

Hearing a scream, then a bang, I ran. Sprinting away from the noises, I entered a deserted garden. Thinking my eyes were playing tricks on me, an alien leapt in front of me. It shot a car, which suddenly disappeared. Snatching his gun, I shot it fiercely. *Phew!* I thought.

Colm Charles David Read (11)
St Swithun's Catholic Primary School, Portsmouth

The Strange Present

It was Monday, the day I hated. It was the usual routine: get dressed, have breakfast, clean teeth, then get the post. Usually there is no post for me, but today there was a giant present blocking the doorway. On the front, it said *'To Ellie'*. Carefully I opened it.

Ellie Dommersen (10)
St Swithun's Catholic Primary School, Portsmouth

Goldilocks, The Three Bears And Emily

Once upon a time, Emily was reading
Goldilocks and the Three Bears.
She had just finished reading the book. She
looked at the front cover and it said 'Goldilocks,
the Three Bears and Emily'
Suddenly, she heard a sucking sound. All
the words from the book hurtled out. Emily
disappeared.

Isabel Flynn (9)
St Swithun's Catholic Primary School, Portsmouth

Stage Fright

Standing up slowly, I felt sick. My stomach was jumping. Below me, I heard voices saying the words practised for weeks. Finally, my chance to shine had come. For once I was the star. Hearing the music I was rushed on stage. I tried to remember my lines and failed.

Ellen Pearce (11)
St Swithun's Catholic Primary School, Portsmouth

Mystical Magic

Taking one last look at his Nike trainers, sweating like a hound-dog, Colm's crooked, beady finger pointed towards the ordinary, mucky, worthless trainers. Under his breath he murmured, 'Cheetah feet, now!' Sliding them onto his feet and looking in the mirror, he saw cheetah spots.
What had he become?

Lillie Boyett (11)
St Swithun's Catholic Primary School, Portsmouth

Lumpty Dumpty Had A Great Yolk!

Lumpty Dumpty sat on the floor. Lumpty Dumpty had a great leap, but Lumpty Dumpty never had a great fall! Well, to be honest, Lumpty Dumpty was never seen again, because the king's knights and horses were on lunch break at the time. So Lumpty Dumpty was never seen again!

Matthew McDonald Woods (11)
St Swithun's Catholic Primary School, Portsmouth

Have You Ever Seen A Dinosaur?

Have you ever met a dinosaur? I have! He was 100,000 years old and still had a dad. He was called Bum-Bum! If you ever met a dinosaur, what would you do? Would you run away scared, or stay for tea? Because he might just be a good friend!

Emily Coomes (11)
St Swithun's Catholic Primary School, Portsmouth

Untitled

Beating down, the sun was at 31°C. I slapped on the sun cream. I wandered over to the ice cream van for a nice, cold lolly. As I strolled back, I couldn't remember where I was sat. I ended up sitting in a lady's seat, but finally I found it.

Luke Simmons (11)
St Swithun's Catholic Primary School, Portsmouth

Funfair

Exciting as it was, on a scorching hot day, we were going to the funfair. I strolled over and went over to the curling candyfloss maker and my tummy rumbled. I thought to myself, *let it melt in my mouth, let it taste so divine, as making me sticky.*

Sophia Molloy (9)
St Swithun's Catholic Primary School, Portsmouth

231

Magic Hat

My younger brother, Bob, is a pain. He takes all
my stuff. Worse yet, Mum never tells him off!
I went off with my friend, Finton, not my
annoying brother.
'Look, a hat!' Finton climbed the tree to get it
for me.
'It's magic, thank you so much.' I replied.

Alan Blake (10)
St Swithun's Catholic Primary School, Portsmouth

School

I sat waiting, waiting. Nothing moved. Everything was quiet. What was that? It seemed to be coming nearer. My doom was approaching. All hope of safety was disappearing. I desperately tried to hide. Everything was hopeless. The door opened …
'Hi, Jess!'

Cecilia Dunhill (9)
Skippers Hill Manor Preparatory School, Mayfield

The End Of The World

The sun was big. Seventy-two times bigger.
The sky was red and there was no sound but
the burning of trees. It was sad, very, very sad.
People and animals were burning up. It was
very, very sad. It was the end of the world!

Isaac Swirsky (9)
Skippers Hill Manor Preparatory School, Mayfield

The Worst

I peered through the bars. The horror struck my eyes. She was there, carrying me into the dark room. I closed my eyes. She pulled me out from the cage. I hissed and snarled. I lunged at the vet, my claws out. I scratched her leg and ran.

Sam Steward (8)
Skippers Hill Manor Preparatory School, Mayfield

The Giant Squid

The submarine was cold. Tom was driving along. He saw something that was big, black and dark, a big fish. It got closer. Tom was scared. It was a squid, a giant squid. Tom was very excited! Yippee! He took a photo. It zoomed off. He never saw it again.

Bertie Cook (9)
Skippers Hill Manor Preparatory School, Mayfield

The Vets

The dragon hissed through the bars of the cage. Bottles of medicine, glinting knives, white-washed walls, a skeleton.
Hiss! Spit!
The knife came closer.
Miaow!
The knife was struck.
'Be still my cat!' said Mum.

William Chamberlain (9)
Skippers Hill Manor Preparatory School, Mayfield

237

The Lonely Monkey Finds A Friend

The monkey was in the woods. He got really scared, but it was his birthday. His friend fell down from a tree and said, 'Boo!'
It was a great birthday. He was not lonely anymore. His friend gave him a racing car. It was great. They were best friends.

Emmy Redman (9)
Skippers Hill Manor Preparatory School, Mayfield

The Fat Fish

On Monday, I went to the pet shop. Mum said I could get a pet. I wanted a fish. I chose the fattest one. I named it Flapper. I have no idea why, but I liked it. On the way home I bought a fish tank with coral in it.

Olivia Deeprose (9)
Skippers Hill Manor Preparatory School, Mayfield

Hairy And Scary

The hairy scary monster rose up in front of her,
his eyes burning like fire. He was going to get
back his revenge. His mouth opened to reveal
his sharp teeth. He was going to roar.
'Give me back my toy!' shouted her brother.

Emilie Stone (9)
Skippers Hill Manor Preparatory School, Mayfield

The Best Fighter Ever

Jimmy awoke one morning. To his surprise there, on his tree house table, was a voice recorder. The recorder was blackmailing him into giving them his priceless weapon - the Master Sword. When used, its owner would always win any fight.
'Jimmy, have you finished your maths exam?' said Mrs Foden.

Benjamin Poon (10)
Skippers Hill Manor Preparatory School, Mayfield

War!

It's gloomy. We're losing. Look, there it is. I've got it! I've got to get it in the enemy base. Got past the defence. It's in! Chelsea won the FA Cup against Manchester United!

Leo Flaherty (10)
Skippers Hill Manor Preparatory School, Mayfield

Off To China

Joe was flying to a far-off land, China. Looking down, he saw his house, Butter Cottage. It was a lovely day and he felt like some tea.
'OK, I've landed.'
'Oh no! Don't squash me!'
Squat!
'I got the fly, Mum!' said the boy.

Charlie Scates (10)
Skippers Hill Manor Preparatory School, Mayfield

Imagination

Screech!
What was that? Is it a monster?
Bang!
Now it's at the door! Is it a burglar? Is it a
bogeyman? Or Dracula? Or … ?
Thud!
It's coming up the stairs.
Squeak!
It's coming along the landing.
Creak!
It's opening my bedroom door …
'Night, night, Jimmy!'

Olly MacKenzie (10)
Skippers Hill Manor Preparatory School, Mayfield

The Magical Triangle

I decided to go on a boat trip with my brother. We sailed the Atlantic. Sadly, we went through the Bermuda Triangle. I luckily got out quick enough, but my brother didn't. I was just about to go under for the last time, when someone whispered,
'This is your level.'

Robert Ellis (10)
Skippers Hill Manor Preparatory School, Mayfield

The Monster

I stared down at the loch. Something moved. A black shape loomed into view, then moved out of sight. I ran down to the loch and jumped in. when I surfaced, something pulled me down. Everything went black. The blackness never ended.

Cameron Carr (10)
Skippers Hill Manor Preparatory School, Mayfield

Shark

I opened my eyes. There were fish swimming around me. I saw a dark shape in the distance. It was coming closer. I realised what it was. *Shark!* I swam faster. Why was it chasing me? I looked behind me.
Bang! I woke up. It was a dream.

Martha Reynolds (10)
Skippers Hill Manor Preparatory School, Mayfield

Me And My Thoughts

I looked around. It was unnaturally quiet and dark, even for where I was. Suddenly, there was a flash and a figure appeared. It began to chase me. It came closer and closer. I sat up screaming, back in my own bedroom.

Emily Webb (11)
Skippers Hill Manor Preparatory School, Mayfield

Cliffhanger

Jane stood at the edge of the rocky cliff, her red hair whipping against the wind and blood swept across her face. She took a breath and gently stepped off the cliff, into the heated ravine of lava. As the story goes, she was never seen again!

Kirsten Sutherland (11)
Skippers Hill Manor Preparatory School, Mayfield

The Dark, Scary Wood

I was alone in a big, dark wood. I heard a crack. There was something with me. I suddenly saw the leaves rustle. I heard another crack. The creature started running towards me, wailing. It was only my mini puppy yapping and licking my leg in the park.

Marella Reis (10)
Skippers Hill Manor Preparatory School, Mayfield

Three Pigs Go On Holiday

One day, three pigs were walking home. They stopped because they saw a shop called 'Camping'. So the three pigs went inside and saw an amazing tent. They bought it and went camping.

Meanwhile, their mother was having a heart attack because they didn't say where they were going.

Caroline Blaxland (10)
Skippers Hill Manor Preparatory School, Mayfield

The Story About Interruption

There was a boy.
'Mum, I'm stuck!'
'Hey you, stop interrupting …'
'Where are you?'
'I did tell you, be quiet …'
'So, this boy was …'
'In my bedroom.'
'Ssh … !'
'What honey?'
'So he was …'
'My homework doesn't make sense.'
'OK, so …'
'So Dad, what's the rugby score?'
This never ends!

Laura Broad (9)
Skippers Hill Manor Preparatory School, Mayfield

The Ride To Hell

I was falling down through the hard, brown earth. I felt like I was being pulled to the depths of the world. Hands grabbed me, pulling and stretching my arms. I was scared. I fell, on and on. I landed with a hard thud, in the heart of screaming Hell.

Charlotte Collins (11)
Skippers Hill Manor Preparatory School, Mayfield

Nothing But Love

I met him in the park. I fell into his arms. We
danced. Our feet were swollen. He took my
hand and whispered to me, 'I love you.'
I whispered back, 'I love you.'
His hand touched my cheek. He came closer.
His lips were near mine. Suddenly …
'Angie! School!'

Victoria Hurel (11)
Skippers Hill Manor Preparatory School, Mayfield

Scaredy-Cat

I felt him breathing over me. He was trying to tell me something. I felt scared. My hair was sticking up like lasers. I was still in bed. Sweat dripped down my face. What was it? What? It smelt like cat food!
Suddenly I turned round. It was my kitty.

Rory Holmes (7)
Sussex Road Primary School, Tonbridge

255

Moving House

Dear diary.
I got home after school. I saw lots of boxes full of our stuff. It was a mess. I shot up to my new bedroom. It was tiny. Could I fit all my toys in? I really like the pantry and garden. I think I will be happy here.

Rebecca Holman (7)
Sussex Road Primary School, Tonbridge

Alien Disaster

Crash! went the spaceship on the earth. Down fell an alien and died. Along came his friends, collected the spaceship, though the buttons had gone a little crazy, landed it on the alien's grave. Suddenly, the earth moved. The alien popped up in rage, 'Who disturbed my death?'

Milly Rawsthorne (7)
Sussex Road Primary School, Tonbridge

Rush To The Loo

An amazing thing happened when I was two.
There was a rumbling in my rear. I desperately
needed the loo.
'Mum!' I screamed.
'What is it dear?'
That was it. I started to groan. I leapt straight
onto the greasy seat. 'Oh my …' I potty trained
myself on my own!

Areeb Zar (11)
Westbourne Primary School, Sutton

Alive Today

Oh no! Where am I? There is a … er . . don't know. Long green things. As I struggle to get through, I suffer from the lack of air. *Argh!* It's a hideous hairy monster! I've got to get away! Now I've grazed my knee. Oh, it's my dad.

Karan Sritharan (11)
Westbourne Primary School, Sutton

The Nightmare Journey

My teeth chattered as the sweat on my brow dripped down my face. My stomach was a knot. There, in the darkness, was a shadow. It moved forward.

'Help!' I screamed.

'Wake up, Beth! You've got school!'

'OK, Mum.' I yawned.

Leigh McKenna (11)
Westbourne Primary School, Sutton

Alien Disaster

Tom and Tim were playing in the garden, when an alien flew down to them.
'I am going to kill you!' said the alien menacingly.
Tom ran into the house crying … and fainted.
Tim stayed where he was. The alien shot Tim apart. Blood spurted everywhere, as it ate him.

Shaun Clark (10)
Westbourne Primary School, Sutton

Candy Shop

I went into a candy shop. Big and round, shaped like a sweet. Yum, yum, yum! There were: big sweets, small sweets, sour and flavoured. Should I buy a big one, sour or flavoured? I know … I should buy a small one just like me. Yum, yum, yum!

Ellie Weaver (11)
Westbourne Primary School, Sutton

The Yeti

'Help!' I screamed. The big, gigantic Yeti saw me high on top of Mount Everest. Then it started to climb. What should I do? I started to throw hard rocks at him. He slipped and fell. He was flat dead. I was safe now that Yeti couldn't get me.

Kieran Wheatcroft (11)
Westbourne Primary School, Sutton

Nathan And The Cupboard

'Nathan, you cleaning your room?'
'Yes!' shouted Nathan.
He went to push his stuff into his cupboard. He fell through into the frozen wasteland. He went up to a person, but couldn't understand him, but as he ran back, the portal closed and he was locked there for eternity.

Charlie Wright (11)
Westbourne Primary School, Sutton

Aliens

I held out my hand and I suddenly felt like I was flying (but my eyes were closed).
As soon as I opened my eyes and I saw my mum with three eyes. She gazed at me. I went to the mirror and screamed like a girl. My eyes!

Ryan Pennington (10)
Westbourne Primary School, Sutton

Untitled

I was scared. I drew my laser and fired rapidly, then all these other locusts came out of the darkness. Suddenly, a crash! My allies came in and killed all the locusts. Then the mother locust said, 'John, stop daydreaming and help me with the work!'
I'm too addictive!

John Kimber (11)
Westbourne Primary School, Sutton

Good Bad Wizard

'Crochanium!' said the great wizard and out blasted a jet of green light. It shattered the mirror and bounced back, heading straight for the wizard's mouth. *'Ribbit!'* croaked the dumb wizard.

'Nooo!' I begged.

He's not a wizard, now a frog instead.

'Unazandus!'

And he turned back to a wizard.

Uzair Khalid (10)

Westbourne Primary School, Sutton

Creatures And Bullies

I sprinted through the jungle, pushing and shoving my way through. These creatures are vicious. I'm still running and … *crash!*
'What are you doing? Bullying her like that! Come along, Lucy, the playground is no place for you anymore.'
The creatures (luckily) go suspended.

Lisa Abose (11)
Westbourne Primary School, Sutton

Splash

I jumped into the water. *Argh!* I'm drowning! I was spluttering and coughing as I sank down to the bottom of the pool. I touched the bottom. *Phew!*
I was only in a 0.9m swimming pool. I pushed off the bottom and got to the side and climbed out.

Daniel Thomson (10)
Westbourne Primary School, Sutton

The Mannequin

The mannequin moved! It was a bit late (10.30pm) and very nippy, but … that didn't affect my eyesight. I flinched. It moved and I was certain all my hairs on my back (about ten) stood up. Feeling coldness on my shoulder, I stopped breathing … I'd turned into a plastic mannequin!

Lola Oseni (11)
Westbourne Primary School, Sutton

The Yeti

The Yeti was ten metres high and five metres wide. It looked like a gorilla gone super-sized. I was on Mount Everest when this happened. I hid in a cave, but he was there. I saw he was a fake. I pulled off his mask and it was Dad.

Mitchell Deakin (11)
Westbourne Primary School, Sutton

The Phoenix

I strolled around the cave that I found after going down the ladder in the street. Suddenly, I heard the swoop of a bird on fire. It flew into sight. I saw it was a phoenix. Amazingly it dropped a lead. I attached it to him and we went home.

Samuel Kimber (11)
Westbourne Primary School, Sutton

Red Paint

I silently woke up and crept downstairs. The sound was making me shiver. It grew louder and louder. The light was on in the living room. The wall had red paint saying, 'Your family will die today!'
'Argh!' I screamed for my mum and dad. The red paint was right.

Oussama Benlamkadem (11)
Westbourne Primary School, Sutton

Seasick

I grabbed onto something. I didn't care what it was. My head spun round and round. My tummy churned. 'I'm going to die!' I told myself. *Flop* went my body as I slipped and fell on rotting wood. I wish I didn't get seasick on boats. *Splish! Splash! Splosh!*

Nathan Fox (11)
Westbourne Primary School, Sutton

You're Late

'Help!' I cried. It was coming closer. It made a huge, loud noise and was coming closer to me. I screamed. The door opened. It's coming. *'Help me!'* I could not breathe. It's arms were up in the air. I was hiding under my cover. 'You're late!' said Mum.

Ellie Feltham (11)
Westbourne Primary School, Sutton

275

Just A Dream

'Help!' I screeched. It was coming closer. I didn't know what it was. 'Help!' I screeched again. I ran for it. I was really scared. 'Oh no! please don't eat me! I'm too young to die!' 'Wake up! You're going to be late for school. Here's your breakfast. Eat up!'

Danielle Pemberton (10)
Westbourne Primary School, Sutton

A Sunny Spell!

Reading the instructions, Alice prepared her props for a magic spell, 'How to make it sunny'. She began putting the ingredients into her cauldron.
'Lizard's tails, something funny, don't make it rain, but make it *sunny!*'
Bang!
The room was dark. She could hear pattering outside.
'Oh no! Not again!'

Hanadi Izzuddin (10)
Westbourne Primary School, Sutton

An Unexpected Visit

Shivering, Mike stepped cautiously into
the spine-tingling wind awaiting a delivery.
Suddenly, a spaceship came zooming through
the mist and an unusual alien stumbled across,
towards Mike.
'Here, inside this package, is something to be
used wisely.'
Mike nodded and tore the wrapping off carefully
and it was revealed …

Winnie Liu (11)
Westbourne Primary School, Sutton

Nanatoo

Naboo stared at the demon facing him, Nanatoo. She looked like a lady. Naboo tried to think of the magic words. Then they came to him. 'Nana, Nana, go away. Come again another day!'
She shrieked, 'Who are you?'
'I'm Naboo, that's who!'
Nanatoo was never seen again.

Gwilym Turner (11)
Westbourne Primary School, Sutton

279

The Haunted House

Creeping along the wall, Emily discovered a long corridor full of bones on its pathway. She was sure she heard howling. *I must be hearing things,* she thought, but it got louder. It came from the dungeons and there stood a wolf. Hungrily he ate Emily up in one gulp.

Wingkei Hoang (10)
Westbourne Primary School, Sutton

The Kidnapper

Rushing home as I was being chased by a man. I was petrified. 'Help!' I bellowed. He grabbed me. Fighting for my life, I broke out. Running speedily all the way home, I ran to my mum and told her. She said, 'Don't worry, it will be fine. OK?'

Daniella Davies (11)
Westbourne Primary School, Sutton

The Storm

Lashing down on us, the rain poured in our tiny sailing boat. I was petrified. Suddenly, there was a crack. I leaned over the edge of the boat. That's when I saw it. A huge hole! We were sinking. The water covered me. I couldn't breath. All around went black.

Billy Fisher (11)
Westbourne Primary School, Sutton

The Awakening

'The Fire Star's here!' people shouted.
Suddenly, the earth started to shake violently.
Gawain had awoken after years of being
imprisoned in stone. The age of the dragon was
back. Gawain was a heartless dragon, if his
heart was stabbed, dragons would never be.
Gawain's heart was the Fire Star!

Hannah Fowkes-Smith (11)
Westbourne Primary School, Sutton

283

Blink

The Doctor sent a coded message saying, 'You blink, you die.'
Sally was at a freezing haunted house, full of statues and the statue killed a man that was blinking.
Thankfully the Doctor came in and used his sonic screwdriver to save Sally.
'Thank you, Doctor, thank you!'

Jake Loadman (11)
Westbourne Primary School, Sutton

The Lucky Escape

'There he is!' someone shouted and James ran. He ran down a flight of stairs and out of a fire exit. James didn't stop. He ran through the shadows, towards an abandoned house. Suddenly, the footsteps stopped. He was inside the house. He shut the door. He had done it!

James Conlan (10)
Westbourne Primary School, Sutton

The Bizarre Experiment

Carefully, he put a blue coloured liquid into a glass bottle. He stirred it for one minute. He added red liquid to the mixture. Unexpectedly, it turned lilac and started bubbling. The lab shook and the mixture exploded into a huge monster. He would never go in that lab again!

Diego Gunawardhana (10)
Westbourne Primary School, Sutton

My Fear Of Heights

My hands shaking with fear and my legs wobbling with terror. My mind got tighter. Suddenly, my stomach got butterflies as I watched us getting higher, deep into the sky. Then, with my feet back firmly on the ground, I wished to never be afraid of heights ever again!

Sinaide Simmons (11)
Westbourne Primary School, Sutton

Unexpected Creatures

Gazing at this monster, I trembled. 'Mum,
there's a monster outside!'
'Don't be silly, love.'
It had green eyes, long hair, chubby face. It was
pale and looked vicious. And it was walking up
our garden path!
'Mum, it's coming!'
'Don't be silly. Don't you know it's Hallowe'en?'

Oliver Redman (11)
Westbourne Primary School, Sutton

Ice-Blue Eyes

The beast was tall and looked deadly. It had demon blue eyes and long nails. I shivered. It was cold and snowing. It looked like an ice sculpture. It pounced at me. I leapt back. Mum called me in for tea.
'You will be late for your fancy dress party!'

Charlie Pappara (11)
Westbourne Primary School, Sutton

289

Revenge!

Wand at the ready, waving it in the air, babbling his spell. 'Slugs!' Sparks flew backwards knocking him off his feet.
Intensely slimy slugs began oozing out his mouth. Laughter filled the air. The slugs ceased after a while, but it was very embarrassing.

Harry Knibbs (11)
Whiteley Primary School, Fareham

All Her Beauty

There she was, in all her beauty. The doll I had wanted for ages. The doll I would die for. As soon as I got home, I started playing with her. She spoke words that shattered my heart. I tried to run, but I was too slow …

Nicole Westley (11)
Whiteley Primary School, Fareham

Starship Troopers

'Run!' We sprinted away from the aliens called Araconid. They looked like massive ants. Long, curved, sharp knives for hands.
An outburst of gunfire was released on the Araconid. Blood splattered everywhere. A bloodcurdling scream and I was being pulled to the ground. Down, down …

Andrew Renfrew (11)
Whiteley Primary School, Fareham

Tidal Wave, Dying Alive

Perched on a golden beach, my hands clenched to the sand, until fish started to flap around. My eyes looked on further. There was nothing but sand, whilst hearing rumbles of discontent. Everyone was running away and screaming, until a sudden, colossal wave shattered over. Wet, dark, gloomy. Can't breathe.

Lewis Mintrim (11)
Whiteley Primary School, Fareham

293

The Golden End

'Your wish is granted!' the genie said.
'Now what shall I turn golden first?' whispered
Richard.
The genie vanished.
'I'll be rich!' he shouted. Suddenly, his nose
became itchy. He put his finger up his nose
and picked it. Richard was still. Silent. A golden
nose-picking statue. Dead!

Ben Richardson (11)
Whiteley Primary School, Fareham

The Beast

He came slyly crawling towards me. His breath smelt of dead pig. The rain battered down his green, scaly back. My throat went dry. My heart missed a beat. Would he notice me? His eyes settled on me. He was ready to make the kill. *Snap!* I was gone!

Eilidh Chamberlain (11)
Whiteley Primary School, Fareham

An Empty Space

I look down. My stomach churns. The ropes
are attached to me as I walk slowly to the cliff.
Edging my way over the top, my rope snaps.
Turning and tumbling down and down.
'Argh!' I awake in the unknown. Dripping with
sweat. All plastered up. Was it a dream?

Lesley Hull (11)
Whiteley Primary School, Fareham

Killer!

'He's coming! He's broken free!' Sam ran.
Fear ate at him. The handle shook. The door
creaked open.
'You can't see me, but I can see you!'
Sam closed his eyes, unaware that the creature
stood in front of him, holding a knife.
This time, Sam didn't wake up!

Ellen Dennett (11)
Whiteley Primary School, Fareham

Yo, Ho, Ho And A Bottle Of Rum

Lightning struck. Thunder roared. The sea was bloodstained red. Waves crashed upon me. Suddenly, a colossal shadow of doom approached and I felt a freezing hand clutch my neck and drag me up to a pirate ship. I grabbed my sword, lunged back and stabbed violently. I am Blackbeard!

Luke Byrne (11)
Whiteley Primary School, Fareham

298

Red Blood

Dead, but living. His name sends shivers down maidens' necks. Here he lays. In a blood-dripping coffin. The only speck of light that enters this room, is from the doorway. The door shuts. He's waking. He is starving for more red blood. Fangs poised at the ready. Run! Run!

Zoë Childs Ford (11)
Whiteley Primary School, Fareham

299

The Lava Lamp

He crept through the hall, into his bedroom.
He stopped dead in his tracks. There was
a strange, purple glow. *What was it?* He
thought. Weird blobs bobbed up and down, he
somehow knew these were his last moments.
That's what he thought … he'd left his lava
lamp on!

Jordan Anderson (11)
Whiteley Primary School, Fareham

Trapped

There was an ordinary guy called Bob. He had a friend named Fred and they were stranded on a desert island. They would do anything to escape, but one dark night, a UFO was hovering over the island. They were abducted with no idea what awaited them.

Alex Gunner (10)
Whiteley Primary School, Fareham

Tresus Vs Cyclops

Breathlessly Tresus rested on a post. It was silent. All that was heard was his heart beating. Suddenly, something rumbled. It was the floor. Footsteps getting louder, louder, until it was in sight. It screamed and charged for Tresus and knocked him round the head. He was dead until …

Joshua Venables (11)
Whiteley Primary School, Fareham

The Plane That Never Survived!

I was in the huge plane! The plane that I
thought would never survive.
Suddenly, everything went black! We started to
plunge. I was terrified. With my sweaty hands,
I gripped the armrest. Then the plane came
down to the ground. It went black!

Jamie Blissett (11)
Whiteley Primary School, Fareham

The Killer Sleepover!

In my bedroom, thick red blood dripped from the ceiling. Famished zombies walked towards me. Closer and closer they came. Saliva dripped from their mouths. Constantly licking their lips. Their mouldy hands ready to grab me. I edged away. I sat up. I hate it when my brother has sleepovers!

Sarah Mott (11)
Whiteley Primary School, Fareham

Blink

Reading this could save your life! They are faster than the speed of light! As soon as you look away or blink, they will come for you. Remember, once you see on, don't blink or look back. If you do blink, death is upon you, good luck …

Peter Crampton-Barden (10)
Whiteley Primary School, Fareham

The Experiment Gone Wrong

Professor Moriarty steadied the misty vial. Just one drop and all would be his: the seas, the lands, the people. The oozing slime slipped onto his finger. Within seconds, mysterious voices echoed in his head, almost like … orders! Something had backfired. Now the world ruled him!

Andrew Chambers (11)
Whiteley Primary School, Fareham

Battle Of Britain

Bombs dropped, guns fired. England was hectic. Air raid sirens penetrated, families ran to Anderson shelters. English planes were down. The storm above was gathering. Planes plunged - German planes. England had won the Battle of Britain. Cheers roared from below, but up above they wondered - what lay ahead?

Jake Hesketh (11)
Whiteley Primary School, Fareham

Howling Hound!

The hound howled and she dragged the quilt over her head. The door creaked open, then creaked shut. Something rose onto her bed. Another howl and her quilt was torn from her. She screamed when the figure started licking her face.

She awoke … it was her puppy!

Georgia Lewry (11)
Whiteley Primary School, Fareham

Killer Cat

My door opens with a creak. I'm lying
underneath my covers. I can hear my heartbeat
and then something jumps up on my bed.
I woke up, it was only my cat!

Max Whittingham (11)
Whiteley Primary School, Fareham

Untitled

'Up and over!' yelled one of the lads. They scrambled up and ran. The lad got hit in the arm and fell back into the trench and sank in the water below.

'Incoming!' shouted an older man. 'Take cover!'

Bang!

Joshua Blewett (11)
Whiteley Primary School, Fareham

The Magic Trick That Went Wrong

'A bit of this and a bit of that. There, that should do it.' The witch explained.
They started to walk around the cauldron. Suddenly, a bird (dying) swooped in, but they didn't notice. They finished dancing, then all at once, they tried the soup. Suddenly, they turned into frogs!

Bethany Chamberlain (11)
Whiteley Primary School, Fareham

Barriers

Imagine, children acting as if you're not there.
But what if you were running, running away
from something you can't even describe.
Invisible? Yes! It nearly killed me! But someone
risked their life for me. Where am I now? Well,
here and there, sometimes nowhere and
sometimes everywhere!

Megan Thomas (11)
Whiteley Primary School, Fareham

Robber Runs Riot!

I was walking home one ghoulish night, when I came across a drainpipe. Water trickled down like many hundreds of people running a marathon. A shadow quickly appeared. I paused, my vision blurred! All I remember was seeing the sun of the morning daylight. The paper robber runs riot!

George Cooper (11)
Whiteley Primary School, Fareham

My Unexpected Birthday Surprise!

Dank day, miserable for a birthday, up steps into house, lights off, something strange - danger! Candle smoke wafting past my nostrils. Shaking, I creep further … a whisper, a bang … schoolbag slips from the grip of my hand. Cowering under the table, the door flings open! Surprise! 'Happy birthday!' they cry!

Olivia Cowell (11)
Whiteley Primary School, Fareham

Untitled

Mark was watching TV. He heard the phone ring. He picked it up, he then threw it straight back down. Then the door knocked. He ran to the back of the room. He was shaking. The door opened.
'Hi!' It was Mum after all.
Ha! The door slammed on its own.

Danielle Whatley (11)
Whiteley Primary School, Fareham

Forest Screams

I was lost! There was no way out! The forest was dark and sent shivers down my spine. 'What was that?' I screamed aloud. There was a rustle in a bush. 'Who are you?' I asked. 'Don't work yourself up, Hannah,' I told myself.
I opened my eyes.
Argh … !

Hannah McMeeking (11)
Whiteley Primary School, Fareham

Abandoned House

He crept into the unilluminated abandoned house. Suddenly, *crash!* Pots and pans slid off the shelves like an avalanche. He froze with fear. Despite the shock, Chris explored until he came to another room. He carefully pushed the door. Suddenly, something leapt out … a swarm of bats!

Samuel Hodder (10)
Whiteley Primary School, Fareham

Alien Abduction

It came down as I was walking to work. A flying saucer! Everybody gathered round it, thinking it would be safe. I entered the crowd. Two creatures came out of the sliding door and snatched one of the crowd … me! They took me and threw me in a cage …

Joshua Dann (11)
Whiteley Primary School, Fareham

Trouble In A Hot Air Balloon

There were three people in a hot air balloon, called Bob, John and Colin. They were having a picnic, when they realised they were overweight, so John threw over a curry. Bob threw over bagpipes and Colin threw over John … *argh!*

Coby Jordan Parris (10)
Whiteley Primary School, Fareham

Haunted House

I went outside. I saw a house (that had never been there) so I walked over to the door. It creaked open … I stepped inside. I saw a chair dripping with blood. I felt sick. I heard footsteps walking around. I slid under the table. He went. I ran home!

Acacia Hayles (11)
Whiteley Primary School, Fareham

Scared For No Reason!

The doorbell rang … my head was throbbing.
I knew that there was a strange man out there!
Suddenly my phone rang … it was Mum.
'Hi! In a few minutes your long-lost uncle from
Asia will turn up, so let him in please, bye!'
I was safe! For now …

Sophie Parsons (10)
Whiteley Primary School, Fareham

Professor Index

In the laboratory, Professor Index was planning an experiment. It was to upgrade the human race! He said, 'I will take over the world! Ha, ha, ha!'

The upgrades of the humans were there, teeth sharpened. If a human was alive, they would hate them.

'I have taken over!'

Zach Ross-Clyne (11)
Whiteley Primary School, Fareham

That Fateful Day At Swanmore

Once upon a time at Swanmore College, the doors banged shut … there was nobody around, except the head of Year Seven. She was so scared, that she couldn't move, until she saw a … vampire! None other than Count Dracula! She saw an open window and she rushed out …

Daniel Cowan (11)
Whiteley Primary School, Fareham

Information

We hope you have enjoyed reading this book - and that
you will continue to enjoy it in the coming years.
If you like reading and writing, drop us a line or give
us a call and we'll send you a free information pack.
Alternatively visit our website at www.youngwriters.co.uk

Write to:
Young Writers Information,
Remus House,
Coltsfoot Drive,
Peterborough,
PE2 9JX
Tel: (01733) 890066
Email: youngwriters@forwardpress.co.uk